SHERLOCK BONES
AND THE
ART AND SCIENCE ALLIANCE

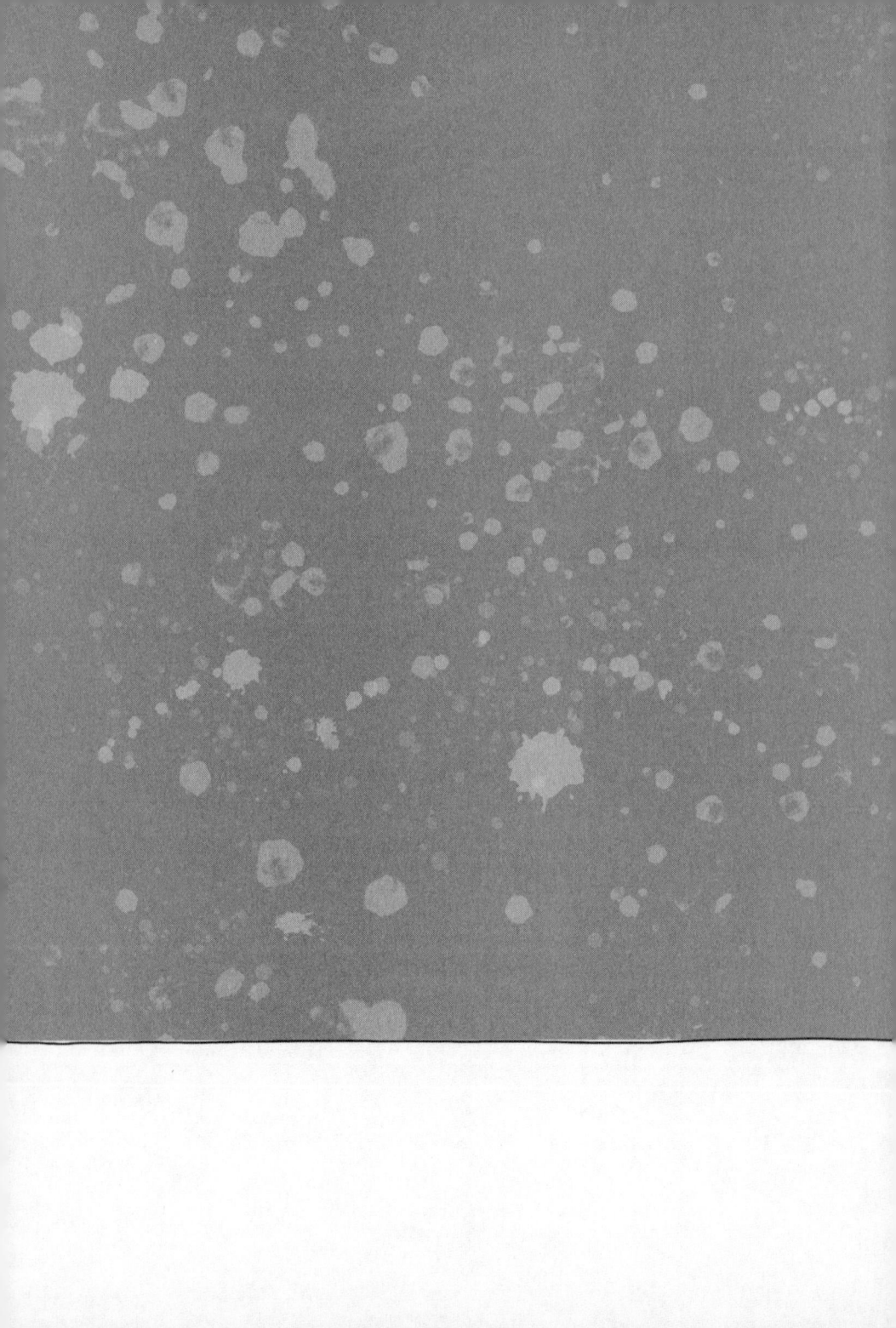

SHERLOCK BONES
AND THE ART AND SCIENCE ALLIANCE

RENÉE TREML

ALLEN&UNWIN
SYDNEY · MELBOURNE · AUCKLAND · LONDON

Dedicated to my art- and science-loving friend Tanny (a.k.a. Cait).

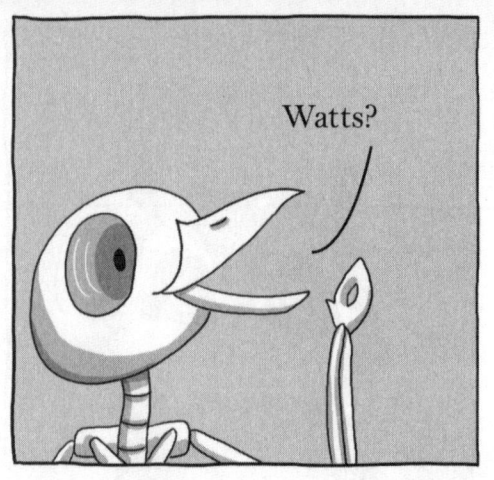

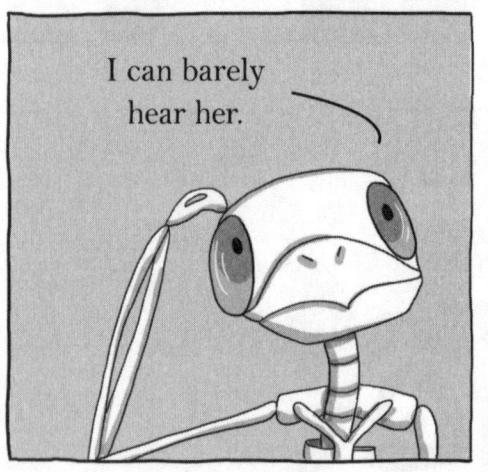

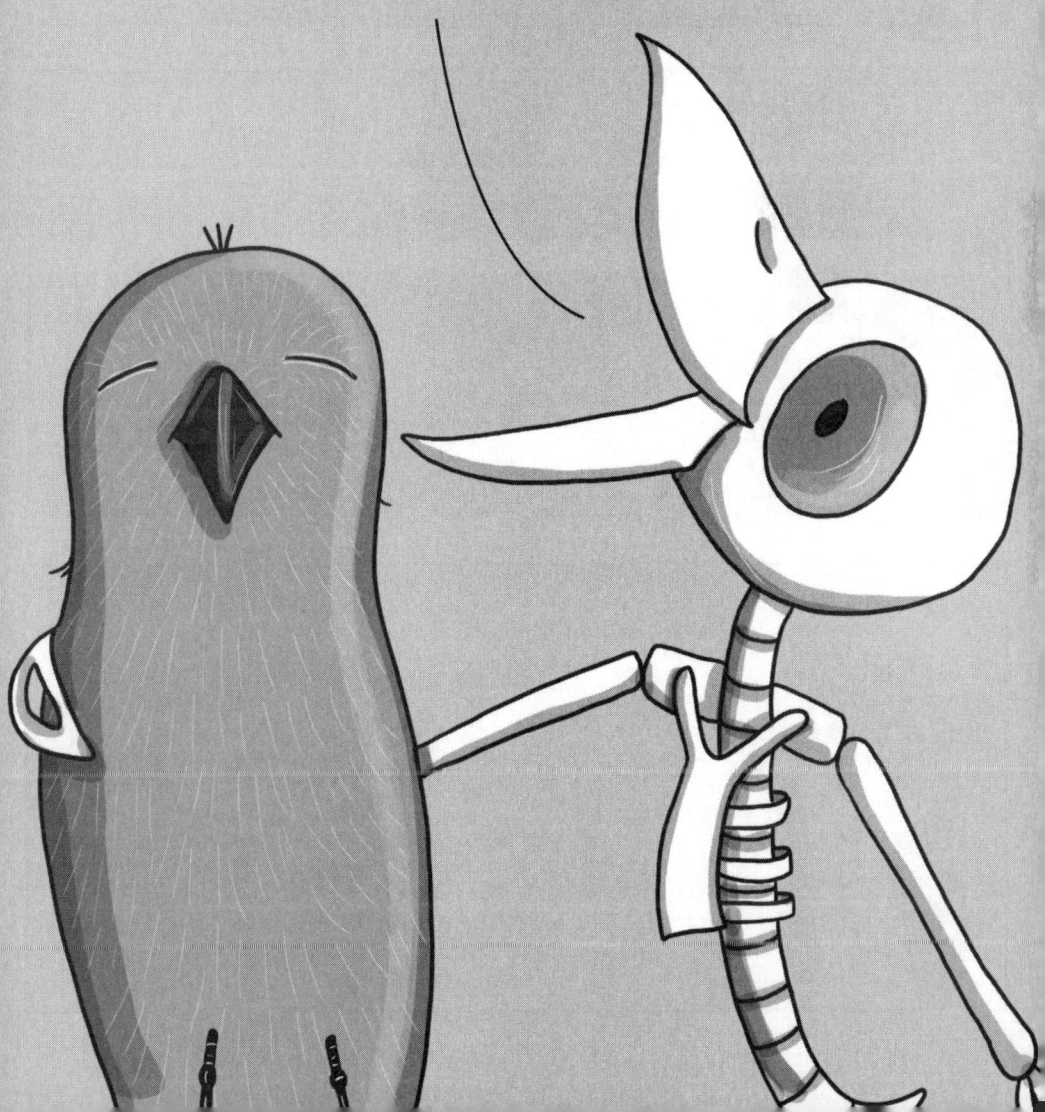

WHAT?
We have art everywhere!

In fact, you can't have natural history without art. Here, take Watts and I'll explain...

Oh no, I'm so sorry about this. Y'all better get comfortable.

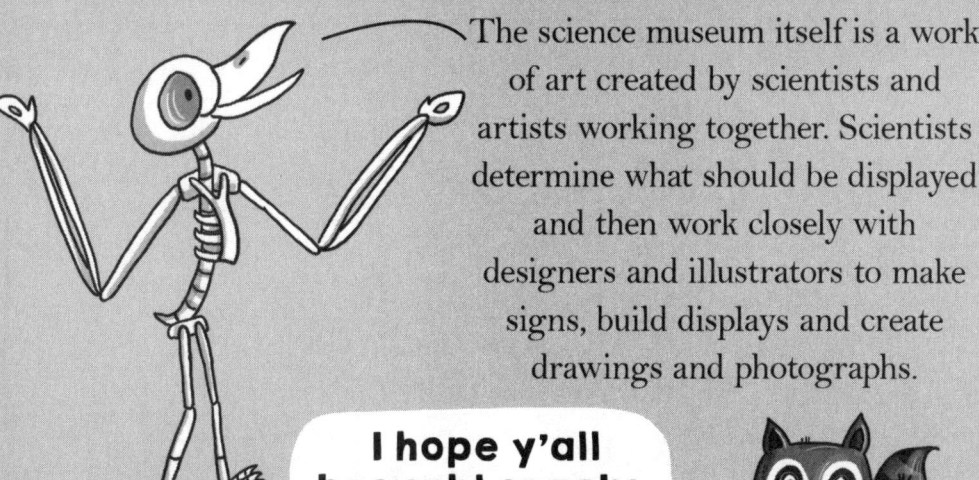

The science museum itself is a work of art created by scientists and artists working together. Scientists determine what should be displayed and then work closely with designers and illustrators to make signs, build displays and create drawings and photographs.

I hope y'all brought snacks. I'm glad I did.

Getting people to understand science takes art. Let's think of the dinosaur.

YAWN. This is making me sleepy.

There are no photographs of a living dinosaur and no one's ever seen one. So an artist works with a scientist to create a drawing that is as accurate as possible.

Now that's an obvious example. But art has always been used to explain the world around us. Think about prehistoric cave paintings that recorded the ancient beasts that roamed the earth at that time. Or the Egyptian pyramids that were built using physics and engineering.

Do you understand, Grace?
Grace? Grace?

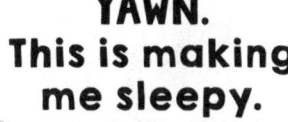

ZZzzzzz

CHAPTER 1
Creep Show

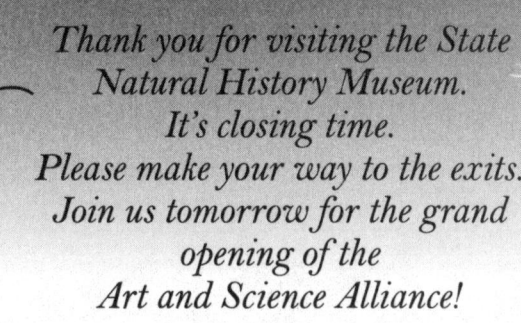

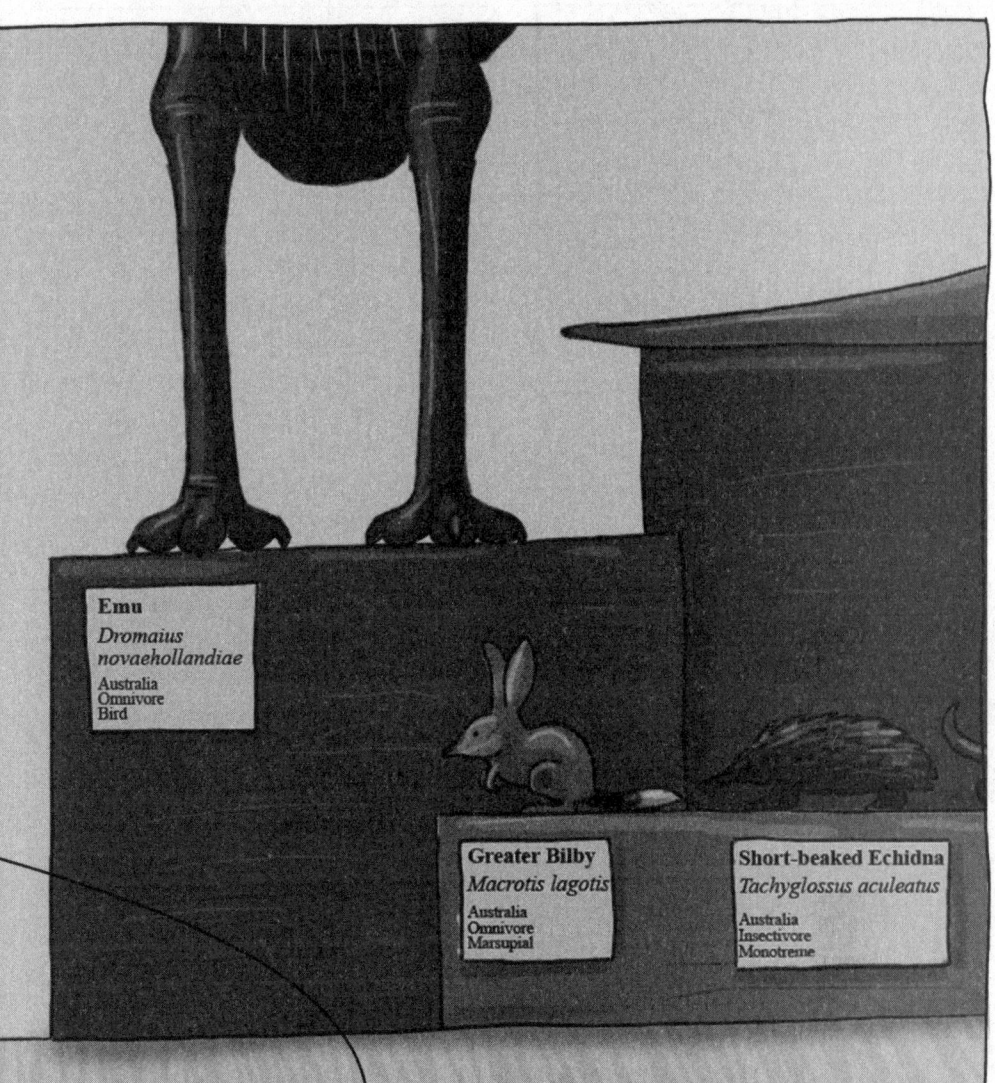

The museum is closed now, so we can have a sneak peek of the new exhibit.

The grand opening is tomorrow!

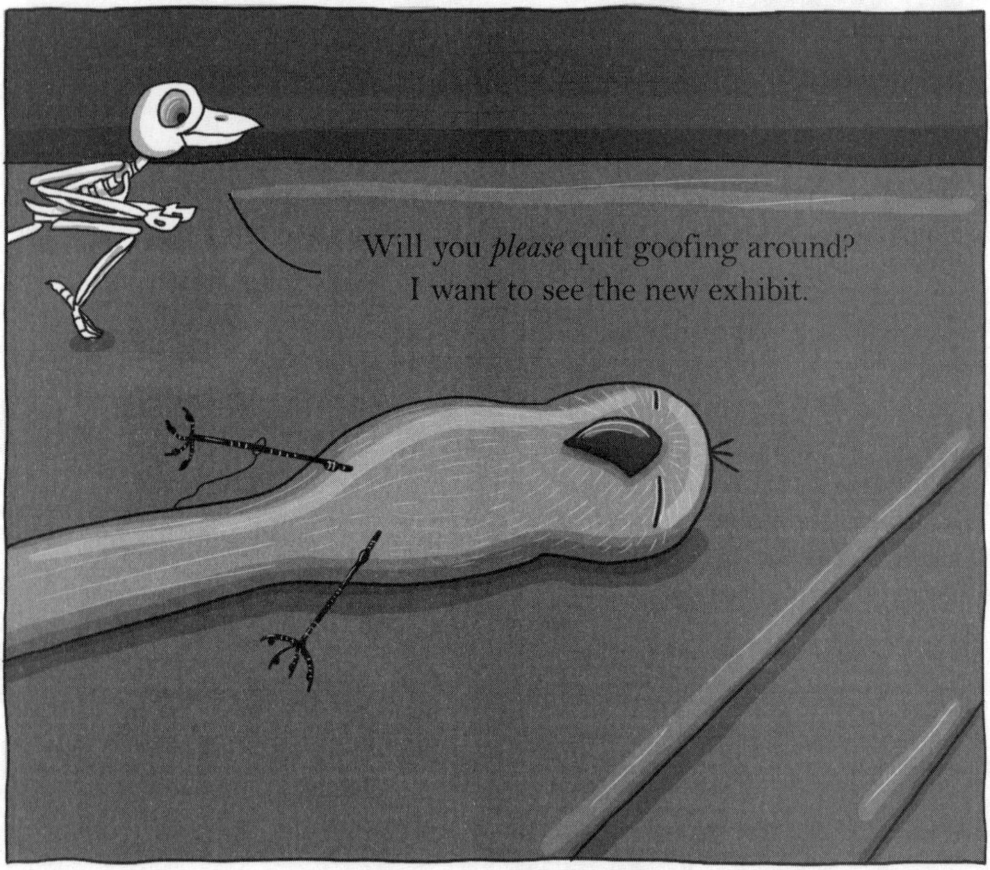

AMAZING!

There were all these **weird stuffed animals** and **giant creepy mites** and monster-sized insect faces.

That's a nice way to put it.

But the best part was the **haunted painting.**

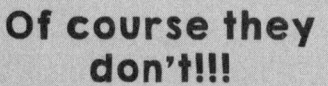

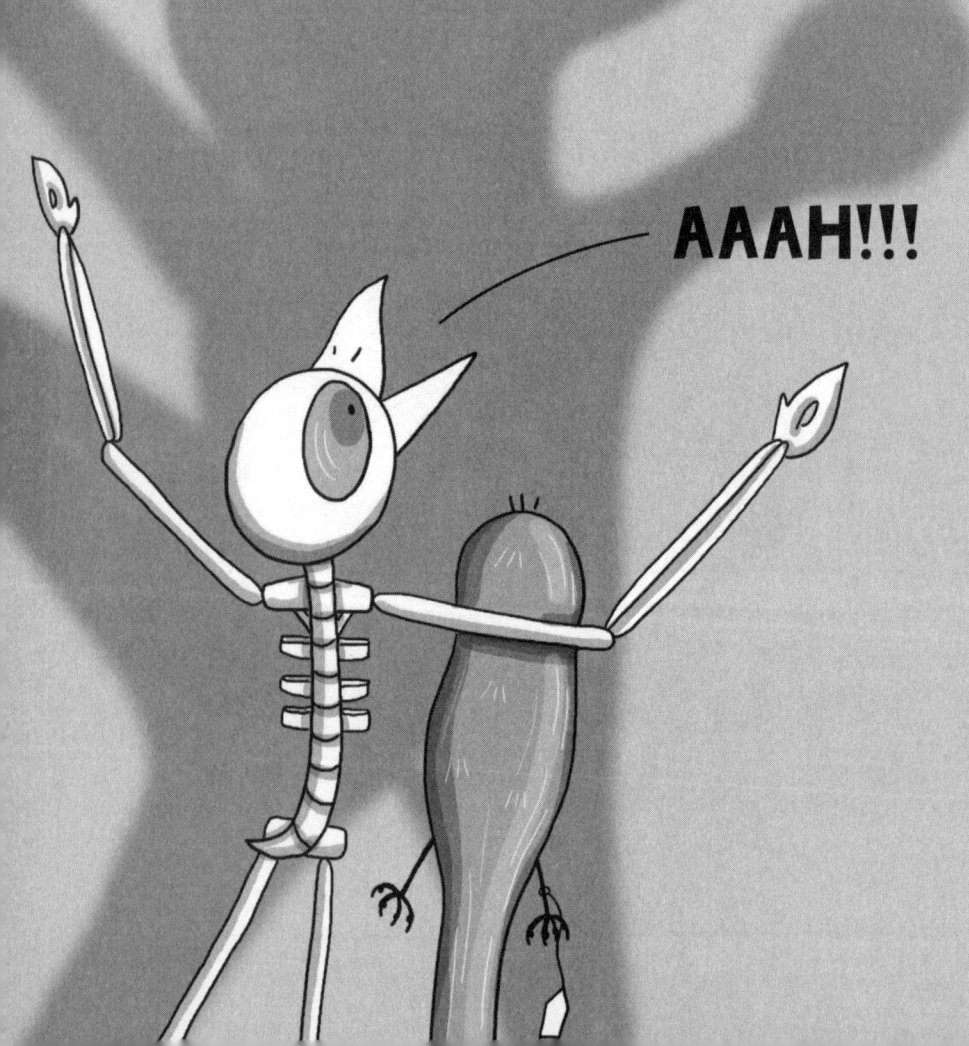

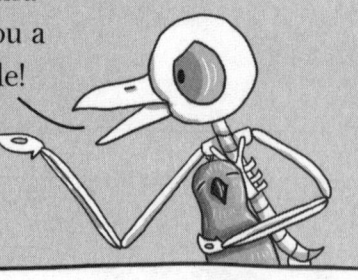

Or maybe someone *who was also definitely not me* broke that valuable tea set and glued it back together with white chocolate, which will be fine, by the way, unless it gets really hot. Or—

It's a ghost mystery.

Boring.

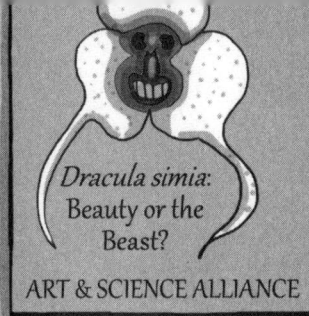

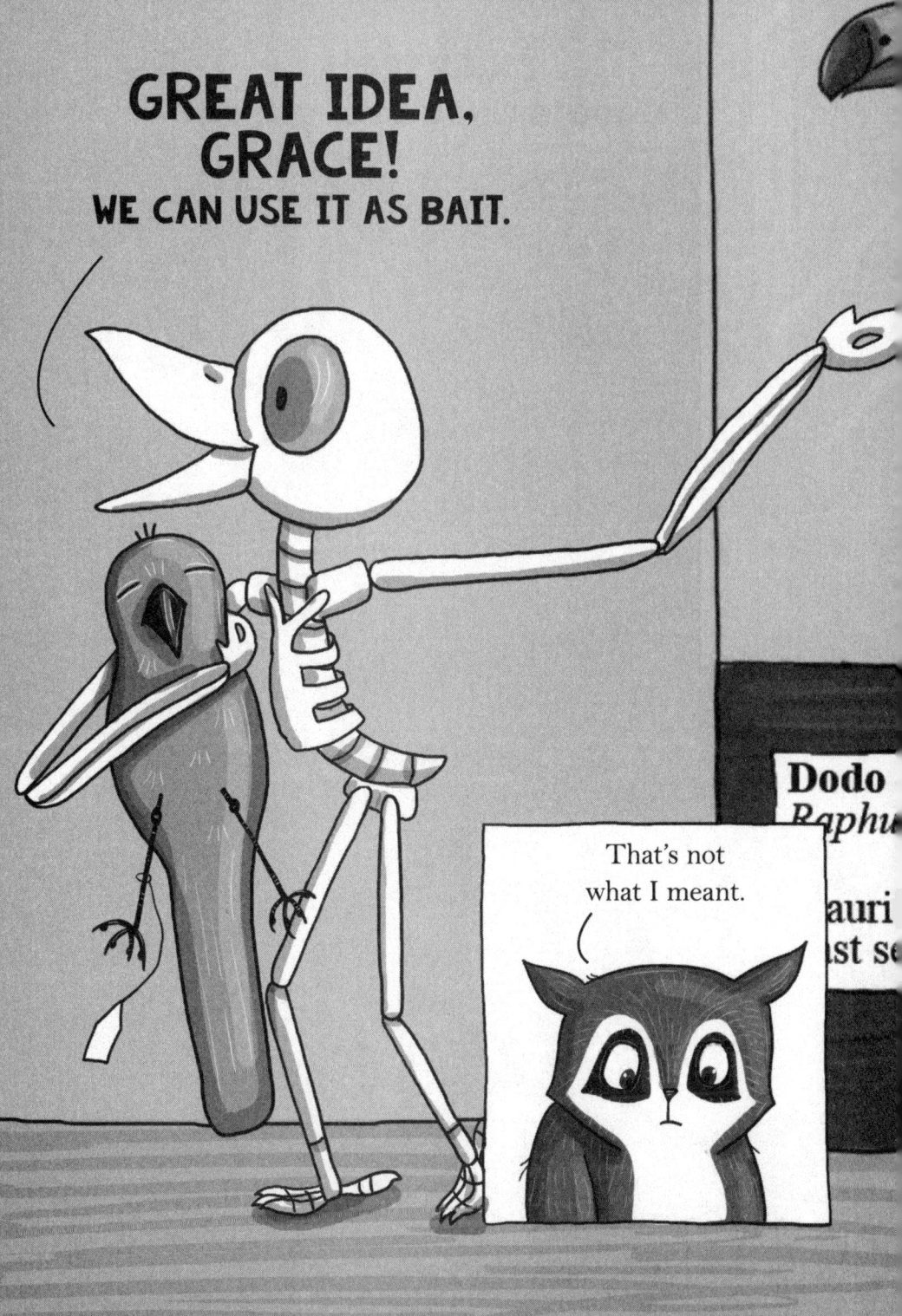

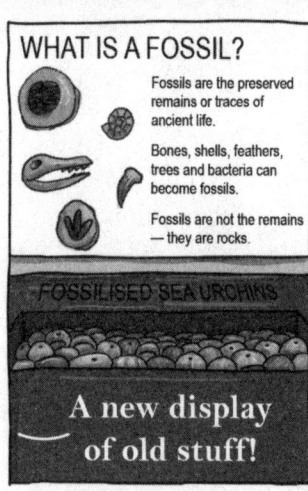

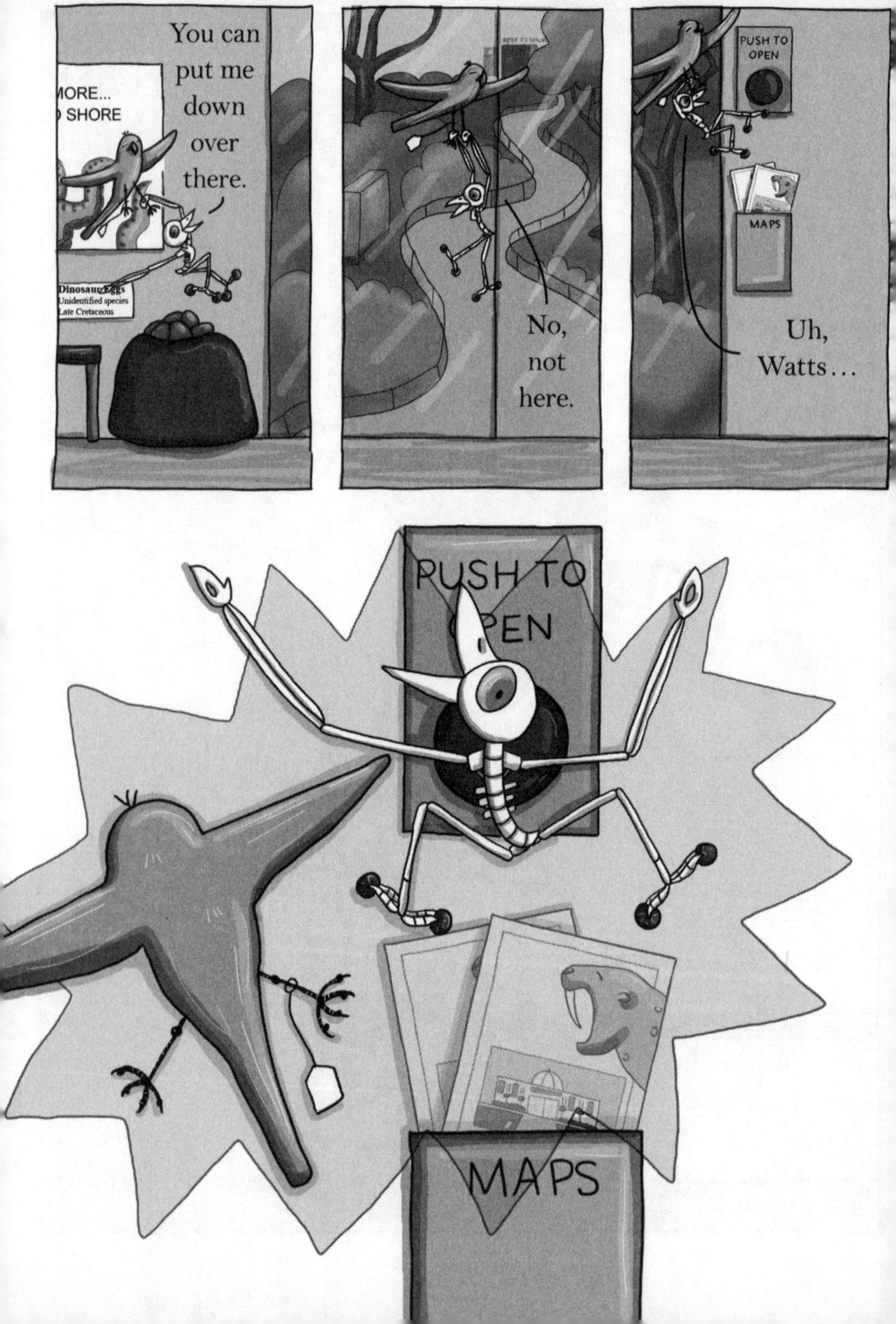

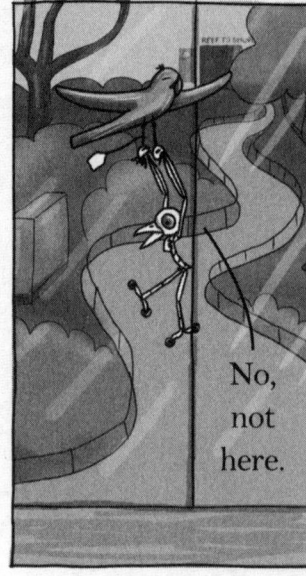

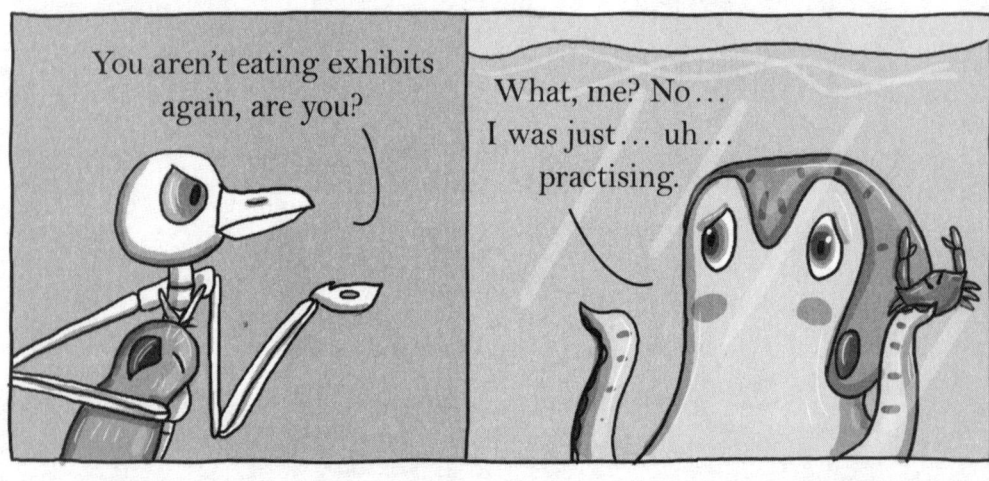

CRASH!!

FACT or FICTION? Is it real or just art?

FICTION — Jackalope Rabbit crossed with an antelope.

FACT — Vampire Deer, Chinese Water Deer, *Hydropotes inermis*

FACT — Aye-aye, *Daubentonia madagascariensis* — World's largest nocturnal primate with rodent-like teeth and a long bony middle finger.

How did we get back into the Biodiversity Hall?

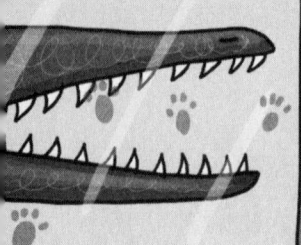

Alligator Gar
Atractosteus spatula
Living Fossil

No, but maybe you are right about the ghost and that's why we're not finding any rats. **I'm thinking it's time to investigate the haunted painting!**

CHAPTER 4
Fright Mite

**EEK!
MONSTER!
MONSTER!**

Settle down, mate. These are tiny little mites, blown up to monster-size. Look, they normally live in hair, skin and fur.

DEMODEX SPECIES
Common mite that lives in hair, fur and skin of mammals.
Microscopic: 0.1–0.3mm

**FUR?
Like my fur?**

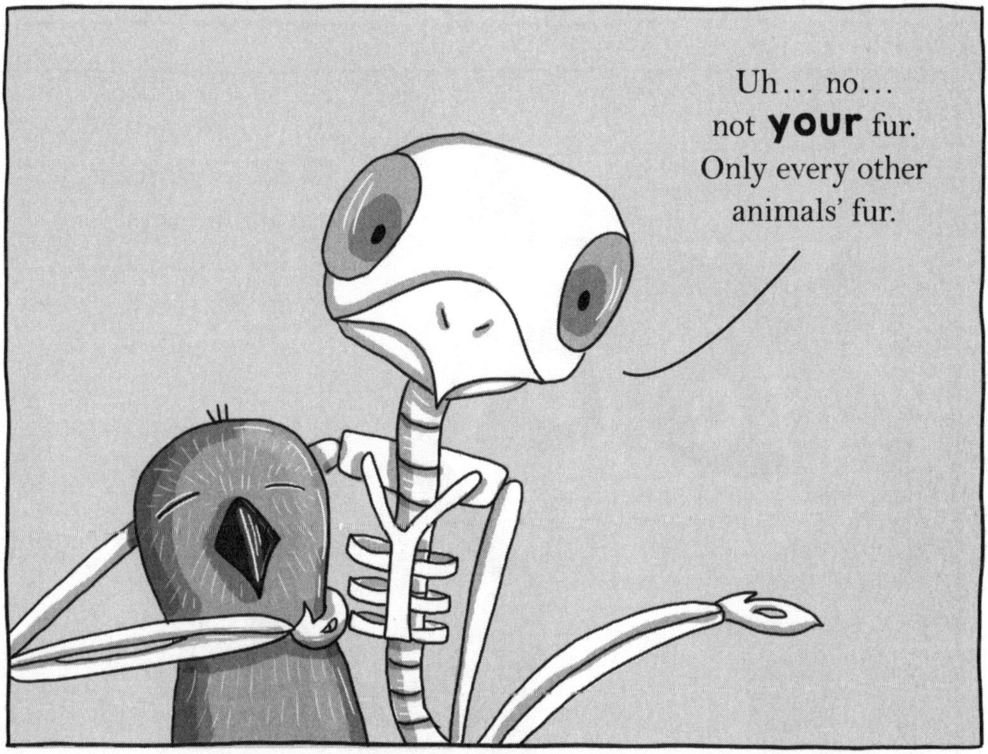

Uh... no...
not **your** fur.
Only every other
animals' fur.

"These would be monsters if they were this big in real life!"

"Now you're thinking like the artist!"

TARDIGRADES
Water Bear or Moss Piglet
Microanimals that live almost anywhere with water.
Size 0.3–1.5mm

"So this artist wants to scare humans. No wonder the security guard was feeling jumpy."

"I wouldn't want to be in here at night either."

ART+MATHS+NATURE
FRACTALS
Never-ending similar repeating pattern.

Fractal-Structure in Nature

Look here to make your own fractal

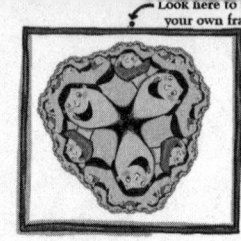

Remind me why we're here again?

To find the haunted painting.

FRACTALS AND YOU

This artwork has placed your photograph into a geometric repeating pattern known as a fractal.

Some fractals have limits to how many times they can reproduce, while other patterns are infinite.

Change a few variables in the mathematical equation and the pattern (and artwork) will change too.

This one looks haunted to me.

The one we're looking for is a painting of a Hydra. The Hydra is—

A beast with many snake heads from Greek mythology. It's so deadly that even its breath is poisonous.

ART+MATHS
HYDRA

A mathematical game with a tree that has a root at the bottom and multiple heads. Cut off one head and X number of heads regrow.

The game is based on the Greek myth in which Hercules must kill a Hydra, a monster with many snake-like heads. For each head Hercules cuts off, two heads will regrow.

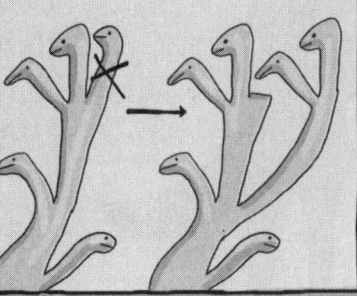

LEGEND OF THE HAUNTED HYDRA PAINTING

While on display at the Royal Museum, several mysterious incidents occurred. Witnesses say the Hydra came alive at night and destroyed exhibits and displays.

While the museum denies that the painting is haunted, they loaned it for inclusion in the
Art & Science Alliance.

LEGEND OF THE HAUNTED HYDRA PAINTING

While on display at the Royal Museum, several mysterious incidents occurred. Witnesses say the Hydra came alive at night and destroyed exhibits and displays.

While the museum denies that the painting is haunted, they loaned it for inclusion in the
Art & Science Alliance.

Why would the museum display a painting if they knew it caused trouble?

I guess it depends on if you believe in ghosts or not.

Either way, it will attract a lot of visitors.

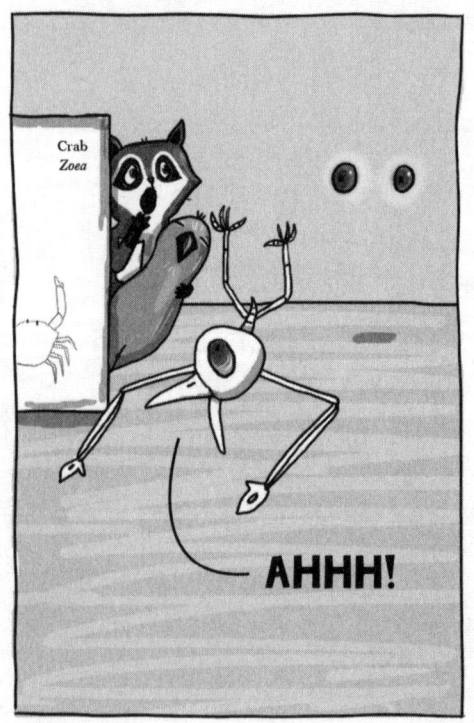

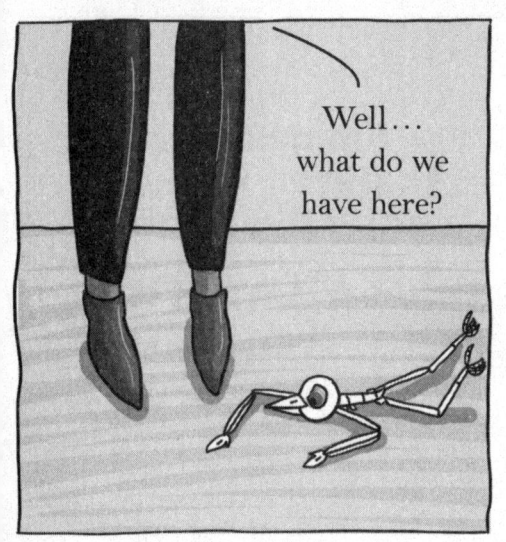

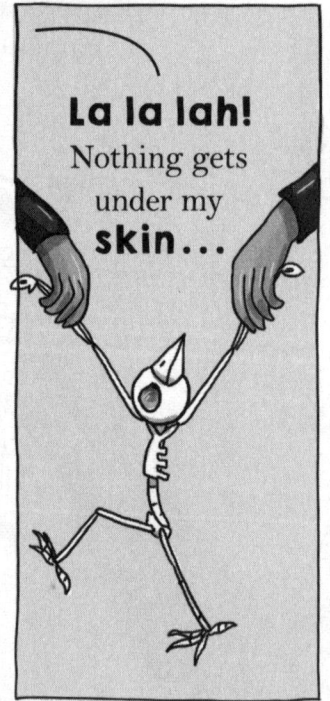

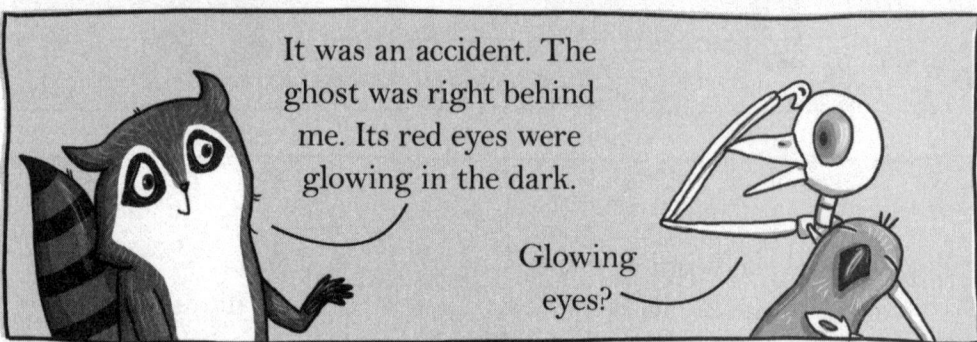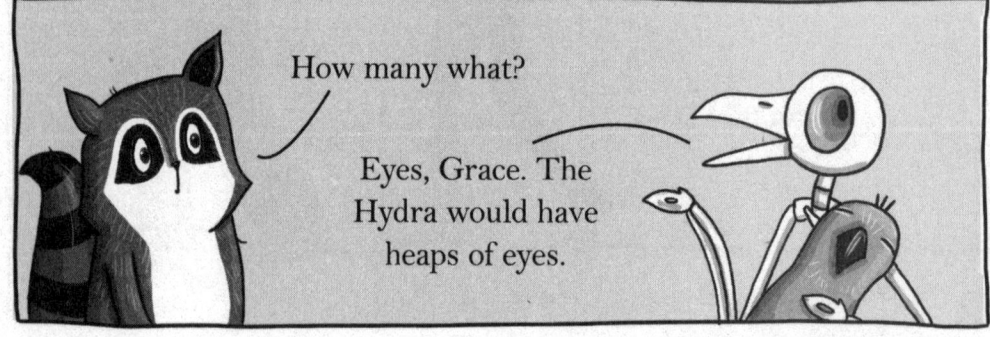

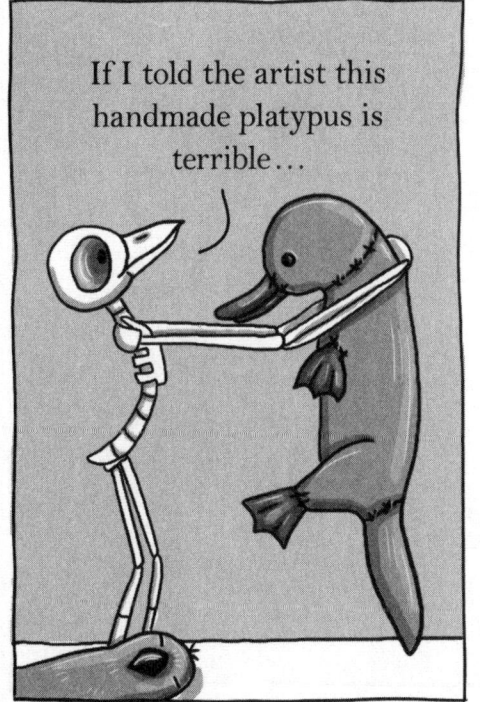

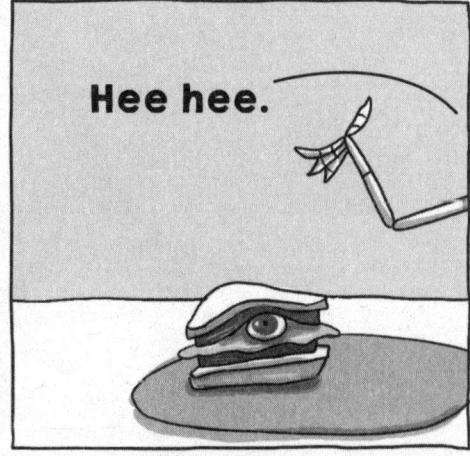

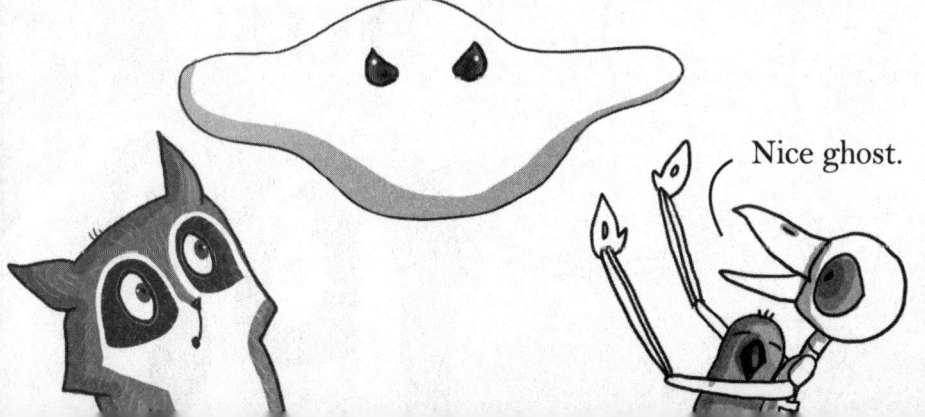

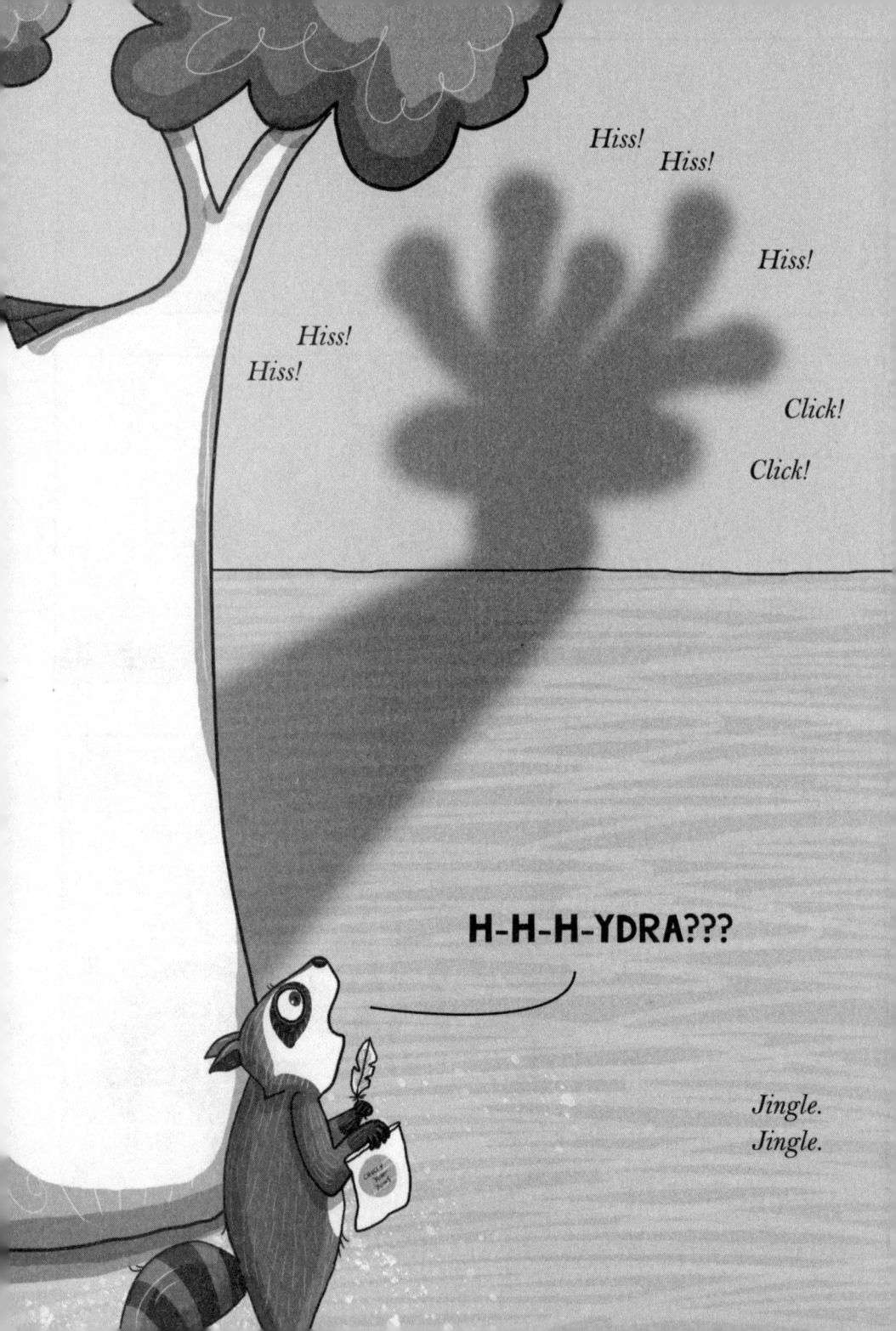

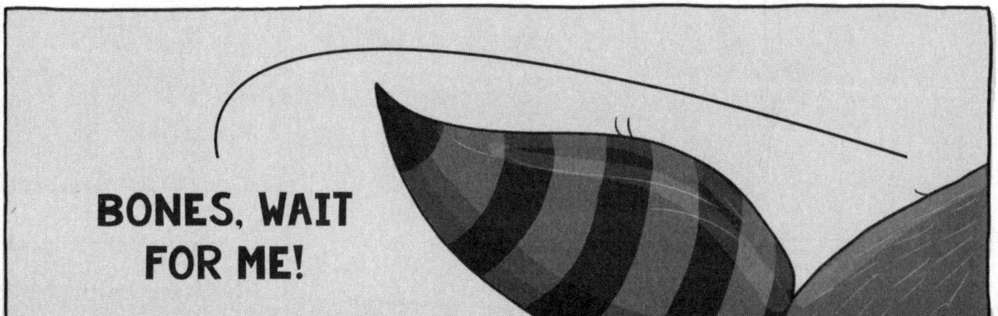

UNDER THE MICROSCOPE

Amoeba: unicellular organisms that are found in oceans, soil, lakes and bodies.

PEDICULUS HUMANUS
Common head lice or louse
Size: 2-3 mm

MICRO-BEASTS*

*Not actual size

SARCOPTES SCABIEI
Common mite that lives in skin of mammals
Size: up to 0.45 mm

Hmmm... I guess you're right, Watts. It doesn't really make sense that the artist would **damage** the art.

Hey! I said that first!

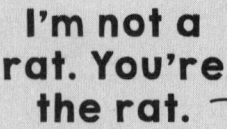

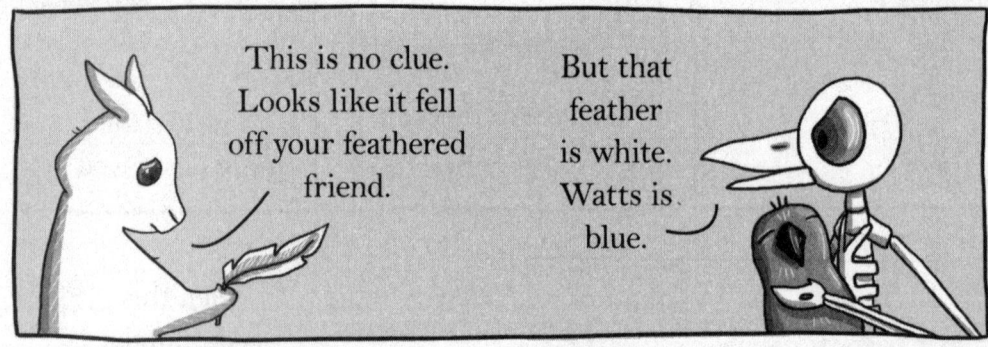

EERIE ORCHIDS

CHAPTER 9
Double Trouble

Monkey-face Orchid
Dracula simia

Monkey-face Orchid
Dracula simia

Hiss…
Hiss…
Hiss…

Well, I'll be a monkey's uncle!

Grrrrrr…

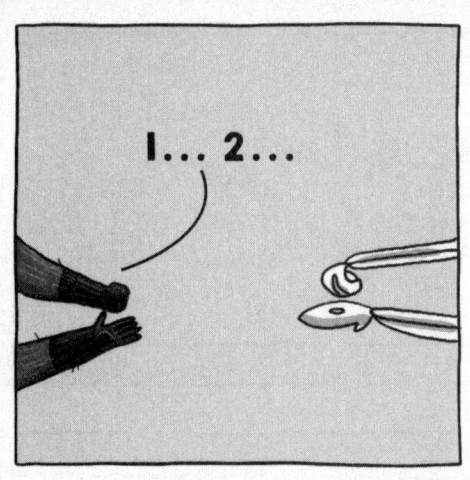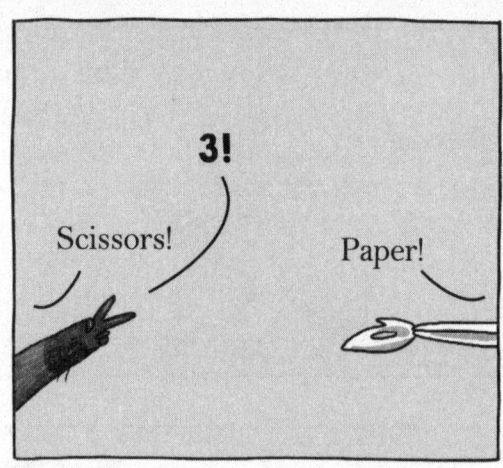

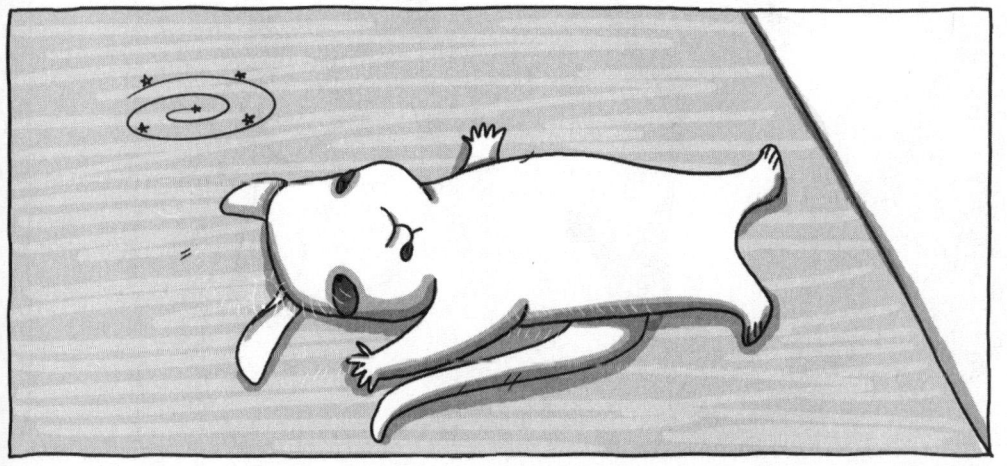

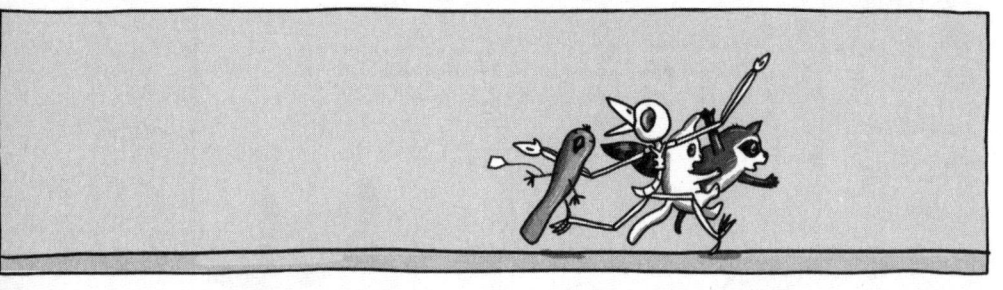
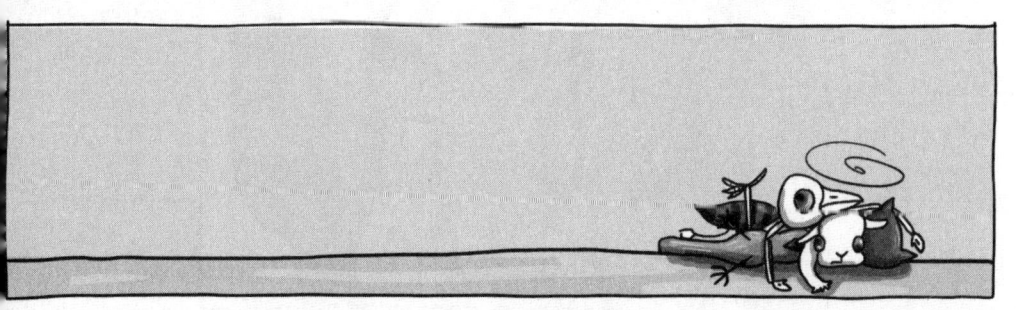

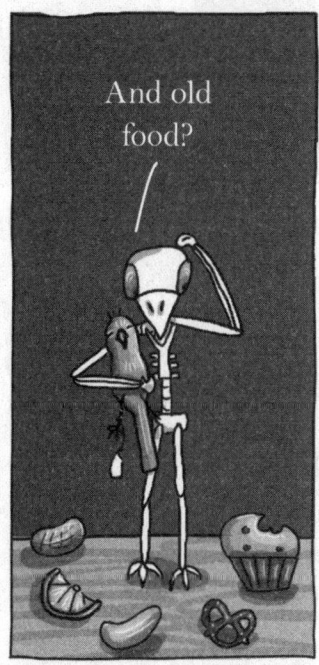

CHAPTER II
If You've Got It, Haunt It

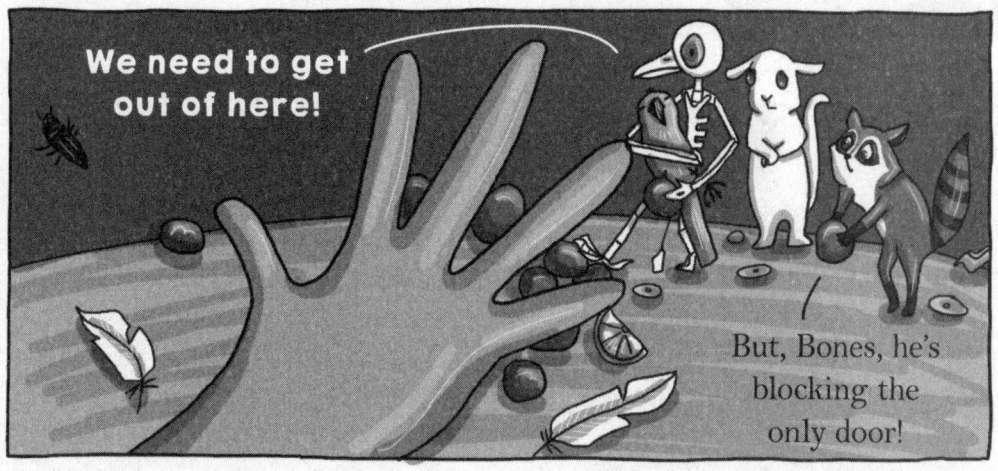

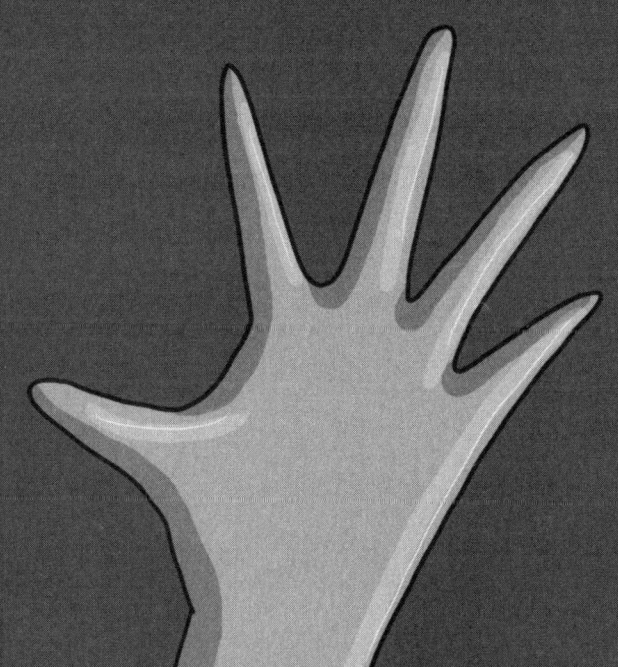

Grab a stick everyone.

Hiss... Click.

BANG!

WE'RE GOING TO FIGHT OUR WAY OUT.

Hiss... Click.

Hiss... Click.

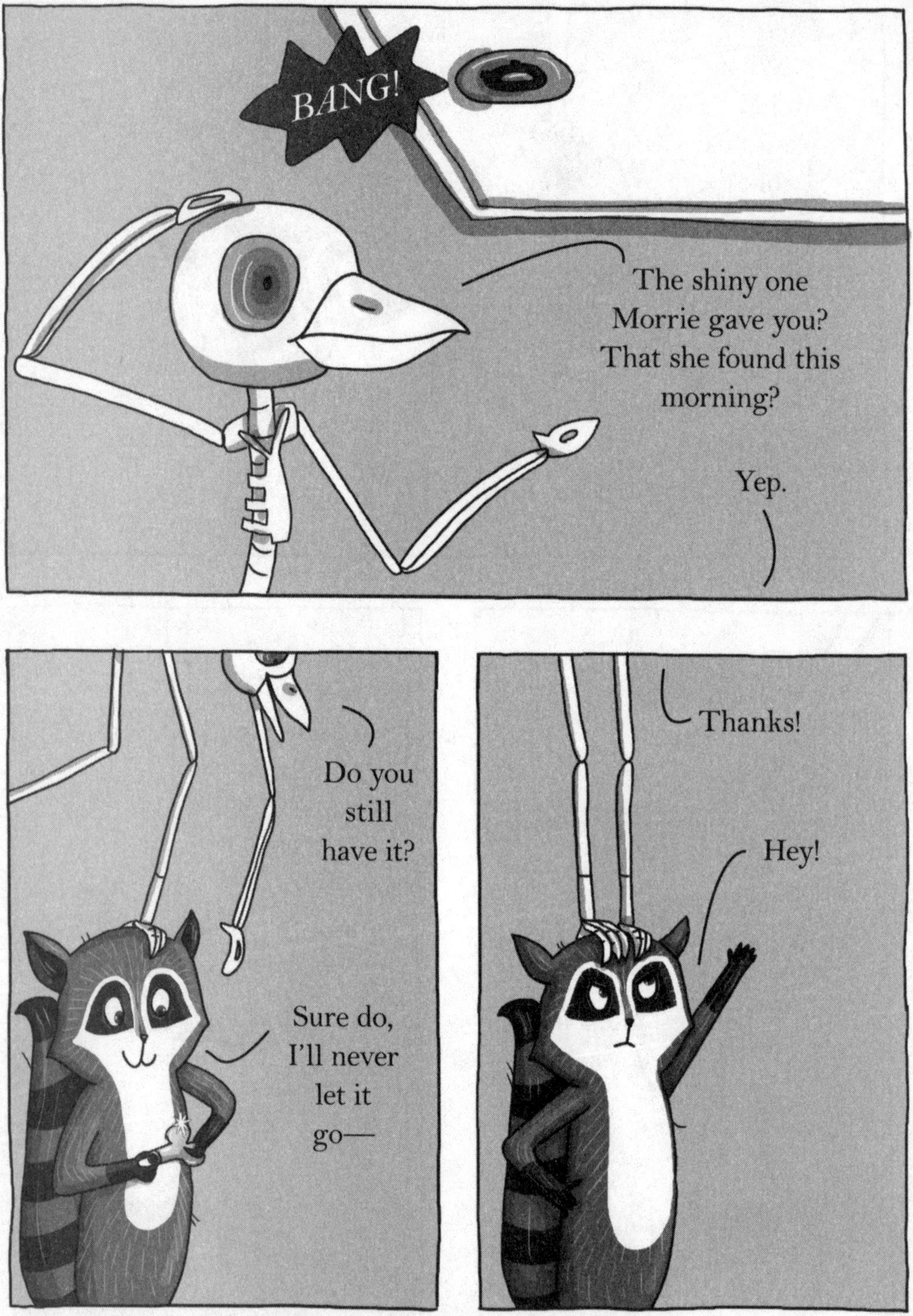

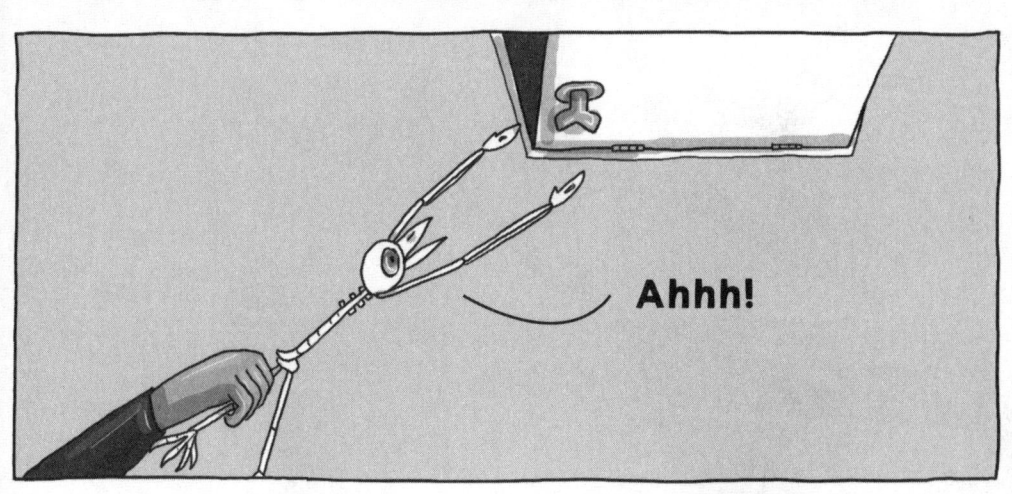

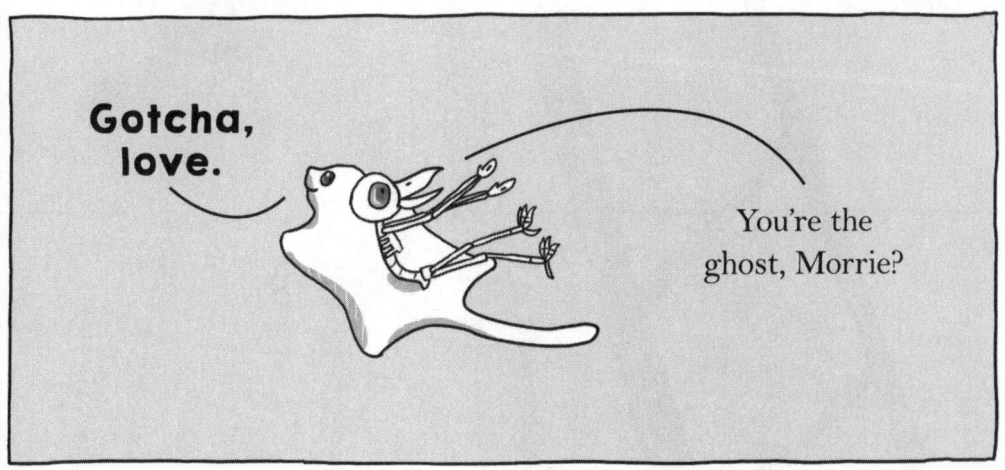
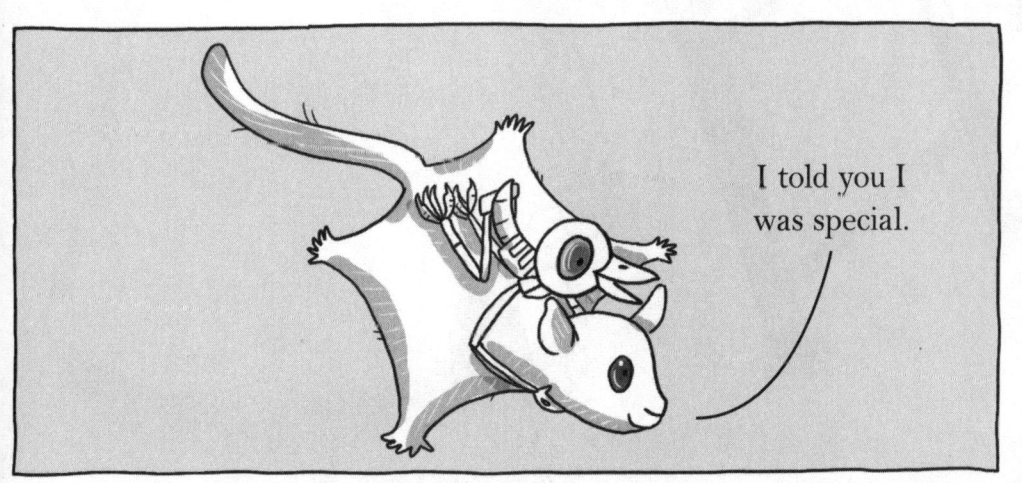

CHAPTER 13
Can't Possum Up

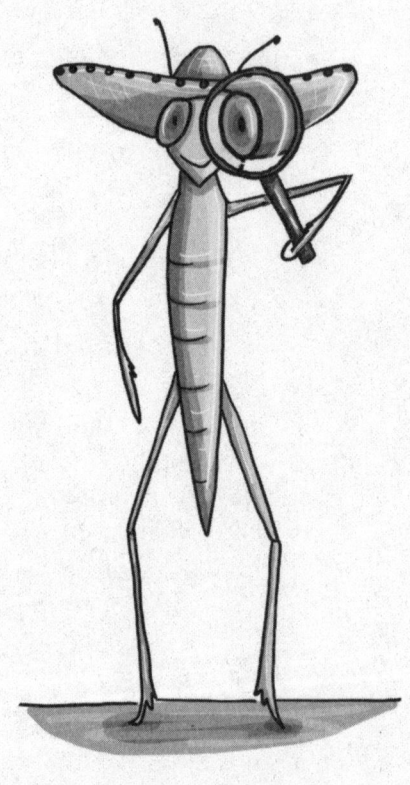

First published by Allen & Unwin in 2022

Copyright © Text and illustrations, Renée Treml 2022

All rights reserved. No part of this book may be reproduced or transmitted in any form or by any means, electronic or mechanical, including photocopying, recording or by any information storage and retrieval system, without prior permission in writing from the publisher. The Australian *Copyright Act 1968* (the Act) allows a maximum of one chapter or ten per cent of this book, whichever is the greater, to be photocopied by any educational institution for its educational purposes provided that the educational institution (or body that administers it) has given a remuneration notice to the Copyright Agency (Australia) under the Act.

Allen & Unwin
83 Alexander Street
Crows Nest NSW 2065
Australia
Phone: (61 2) 8425 0100
Email: info@allenandunwin.com
Web: www.allenandunwin.com

 A catalogue record for this book is available from the National Library of Australia

ISBN 978 1 76106 572 9

For teaching resources, explore www.allenandunwin.com/resources/for-teachers

The artwork in this book was drawn in pencil, then digitally inked and coloured.

Fractal images on p114 were generated with code found at
http://www.malinc.se/m/ImageFractals.php.
and are reproduced here with kind permission from Malin Christersson.

Cover design by Sandra Nobes
Text design by Renée Treml
Set in 13 pt Bell MT by Renée Treml
Printed in March 2022 in Australia by McPherson's Printing Group

1 3 5 7 9 10 8 6 4 2

 The paper in this book is FSC® certified. FSC® promotes environmentally responsible, socially beneficial and economically viable management of the world's forests.

ACKNOWLEDGEMENTS

Thank you to all the wonderful children, carers, teachers, booksellers and librarians who have read or shared my books and offered me encouragement. It really makes a difference. Thank you.

Special thanks to Peter William Popple for assistance and expertise flatting the artwork for this book – you were a lifesaver. Thank you to my agent, Elizabeth at Transatlantic, for everything you do behind the scenes. Many thanks to my writing group for being a wonderfully supportive community, and in particular Kaye, Stef and Michelle for reviewing early versions of the book.

Thank you, Jodie, Sophie and all the amazing staff at Allen & Unwin for bringing the third Sherlock Bones book to life.

Thank you, Malin Christersson, for your generous permission to include a real fractal image from your website – check it out at http://www.malinc.se/. Also, thanks to the Duke Lemur Center in North Carolina for taking the time to answer my questions about the aye-aye (it would have been really cool if they could *actually* pick locks with that long finger – ah well). And, of course, thank you to Eric, Calvin, Tassie and all my friends and family for everything – I couldn't have done this without you.

ABOUT THE AUTHOR

Renée was born and raised in the USA and moved to Australia in 2007. She met Sherlock Bones shortly after arriving in the country – he was posing in an exhibit of tawny frogmouth skeletons in the Queensland Museum in Brisbane. This story was inspired by an albino wallaby Renée saw hopping about the hills of Tasmania... she couldn't stop wondering how it could have survived all those years in the wild being pure white.

Renée's stories and illustrations are inspired by nature and influenced by her background in environmental science. She lives and works on the beautiful Surf Coast in Victoria with her husband, son, enthusiastic little dog and lazy bearded dragon.

A closer look at some of the exhibits

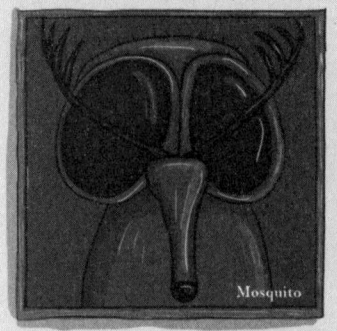

This display shows tiny creatures in ways that are not usually seen with the naked eye.

MICRO-BEASTS

This section focuses on unusual animal traits and behaviours, including a bug who camouflages itself with the bodies of dead ants and a lemur who moves like it's dancing.

Armoured Ball Ground Pangolin
Smutsia temminckii
These animals are not reptiles, they are anteaters that are covered in hard scales and roll into a ball when threatened.

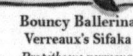

Bouncy Ballerina Verreaux's Sifaka
Propithecus verreauxi
With long legs and short arms, these lemurs look like they are dancing when they move on the ground.

WEIRD, WONDERFUL AND REAL WILDLIFE

Creepy Camouflage Assassin Bug
Acanthaspis petax
Juveniles put dead ants on their back to keep predators away and sneak up on their prey.

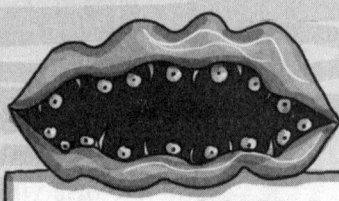

See It to Believe It Scallops - Pectinidae family
These molluscs have 100 blue eyes on the edge of their shell that can distinguish between light and dark.

from the Art and Science Alliance

This part highlights animals so out-of-the-ordinary they could be mistaken for imaginary creatures, like a really cute octopus with 'ears' and a tiny pink armadillo that swims through the sand. The animals shown on this page all exist in real life.

FACT **Bohol Tarsier**
Tarsier syrichta
Tarsiers are one of the smallest known primates, yet they have the biggest eyes and hands relative to body size of all the primates.

FACT **Adorabilis or Flapjack Octopus**
Opisthoteuthus californiana
This cutest of octopuses flattens like a pancake on the sea floor waiting for prey and hiding from predators.

FACT **Pink Fairy Armadillo**
Chlamyphorus truncatus
These unusual pink and white animals spend most of their time underground.

FACT or FICTION?
Is it real or is it art?

FACT **Liger**
This animal is a hybrid of a male lion and a female tiger. These huge cats are bred in captivity and would not be found in nature.